EIGHT ANIMALS BAKE A CAKE

By **Susan Middleton Elya**   Illustrated by **Lee Chapman**

Much thanks to Victoria Wells for becoming an editor instead of a chef.
—S. M. E.

To my wife, Nancy, who bakes with love.
—L. C.

G. P. Putnam's Sons • New York

Text copyright © 2002 by Susan Middleton Elya. Illustrations copyright © 2002 by Lee Chapman.
All rights reserved. This book, or parts thereof, may not be reproduced in any form without permission in
writing from the publisher, G. P. PUTNAM'S SONS, a division of Penguin Putnam Books for Young Readers,
345 Hudson Street, New York, NY 10014. G. P. Putnam's Sons, Reg. U.S. Pat. & Tm. Off.
Published simultaneously in Canada. Printed in Hong Kong by South China Printing Co. (1988) Ltd.
Designed by Gina DiMassi. Text set in Pacific Clipper Medium. Library of Congress Cataloging-in-
Publication Data   Elya, Susan Middleton, 1955– Eight animals bake a cake / by Susan Middleton Elya;
illustrated by Lee Chapman. p. cm. Summary: Eight animals add ingredients to make a cake with unexpected
results. Includes Spanish words, a glossary, and recipe for pineapple upside-down cake. [1. Spanish language—
Vocabulary—Fiction. 2. Animals—Fiction. 3. Cake—Fiction. 4. Baking—Fiction. 5. Stories in rhyme.]
I. Chapman, Lee, ill. II. Title. PZ8.3.E514 Ef 2002   [E]—dc21   00-021393 ISBN 0-399-23468-3
1 3 5 7 9 10 8 6 4 2
First Impression

Glossary and Pronunciation Guide

Al revés (AHL rreh VEHS) upside down

Animales (ah nee MAH lehs) animals

Azúcar (ah SOO kahr) sugar

Caballo (kah BAH yoe) horse

Cerdo (SEHR doe) pig

Cerezas (seh REH sahs) cherries

Cuarenta minutos (kwah REHN tah mee NOO toce) forty minutes

Dos (DOSE) two

El mantel (EHL mahn TEHL) the tablecloth

Gato (GAH toe) cat

Harina (ah REE nah) flour

Horno (OHR noe) oven

Huevo (WEH voe) egg

La puerta (LAH PWEHR tah) the door

Mantequilla (mahn teh KEE yah) butter

Más (MAHS) more

Montón (mone TONE) heap

Pacanas (pah KAH nahs) pecans

Pájaro (PAH hah roe) bird

Pastel (pahs TEHL) cake

Patas (PAH tahs) paws

Perro (PEH rroe) dog

Piña (PEE nyah) pineapple

Plato (PLAH toe) plate

Por favor (POHR fah VOHR) please

Rana (RRAH nah) frog

Ratón (rrah TONE) mouse

Sal (SAHL) salt

Sorpresa (sohr PREH sah) surprise

Tres (TREHS) three

Uno (OO noe) one

Vaca (VAH kah) cow

Vainilla (vye NEE yah) vanilla

Eight **animales**, ready to bake,
get out of bed to go bake a cake.

Mouse brings the sugar, one heavy cup.
Ratón says, "**Azúcar** will start things right up."

Cat brings the butter, so creamy and thick.
"Fresh **mantequilla**," says **Gato**, "one stick."

Dog brings the egg, one **huevo** to beat.
"Hurry up," **Perro** says. "I want to eat."

Bird flies in flour. She brings several ounces.
"**Harina**," says **Pájaro** just as Cat pounces.

Frog brings vanilla,
a deep liquid brown.
"**Vainilla**," says **Rana**,
"best stuff in town."

Horse gallops over, swinging the salt.
"**Sal**," neighs **Caballo**
as he comes to a halt.

Cow brings the cherries—red, ripe, and round.
"**Cerezas**," says **Vaca**, "the freshest I've found."

Pig brings pecans, a big, bursting sack.
"**Pacanas**," says **Cerdo**. "I want a few back."

Eight **animales** stir up the cake.
Now their **pastel** is ready to bake.
The **horno** is ready. They feel the hot air.
Into the oven they place it with care.

They've laid out the tablecloth now—**el mantel**.
And **Cerdo** puts plates out to serve their **pastel**.
For forty long minutes, **Pájaro** sings.
¡Cuarenta minutos! Then the bell dings.

"I'll take the cake out," says **Rana**. "No, me!"
"I will!" "No, I will!" They just can't agree.
"We need the best paws,"
argues **Perro**, "like mine."
"My **patas**," says **Gato**,
"will work out just fine."

She pulls out
    their pastry—
        uno,
            dos,
                tres,
but drops
    the **pastel**
        upside down—
            ¡al revés!

Cake on the ceiling
and more on the floor;
there's even some cake
on **la puerta**—the door.
"Look at this heap!"
says hungry **Ratón**.
"Our beautiful cake
is now a **montón**."

"Well," neighs **Caballo**, "we've all eaten worse."
"He's right," **Vaca** moos. "But bring me my purse. . . ."

She gives cash to **Pájaro**, who flies to the store.
She turns to the others. "Please wait, **por favor**."

"For what?" questions **Rana**, with big, bulgy eyes.
"If I tell you," says **Vaca**, "there'll be no surprise."

Seven **animales** sit down to wait.
Perro holds his **plato**, his cold, empty plate.

Pájaro flies back with a large prickly fruit,
a pineapple—**piña**—bought with Cow's loot.

They slice it in rings and add more **cerezas**.
"It's pineapple upside-down cake. **¡Sorpresa!**"

Eight **animales** cut up their treat.
They saved their mistake
and now get to eat.

Eight **animales** all ask for more.
Here's how they say it—
"**Más, por favor.**"

Eight Animales
Pineapple Upside-down Cake

TOPPING (to go in the bottom of the pan):

8 pineapple rings (canned or fresh)
8 maraschino cherries
8 to 16 pecan halves (or 1/4 to 1/2 cup chopped pecans)
1/4 cup butter
1/4 cup packed brown sugar

BATTER (yellow cake mix can be used instead)

1 cup flour
3/4 cup white sugar
1/2 teaspoon salt
1 teaspoon baking powder
2/3 cup milk
1/3 cup butter
1 egg
1 teaspoon vanilla

Preheat oven to 350° Fahrenheit.
In a 9" x 13" baking dish, arrange the eight pineapple rings on the
bottom. Put one cherry in the center of each ring. Place the pecans
around the edges of the rings.

Melt 1/4 cup butter in a small glass bowl for 30 seconds in the
microwave. Stir in the brown sugar. Pour the mixture over the
pineapple rings. Set dish aside.

In a medium bowl, mix the flour, sugar, salt, baking powder, milk, 1/3
cup butter, egg, and vanilla. Beat for three minutes with a mixer. Then
pour the mixture over the pineapple in the baking dish. Bake at 350°
for 35 to 40 minutes. Let the cake cool. Cut into pieces and flip them
onto serving plates, or flip the entire cake over onto a serving platter
and slice.

You don't have to drop the cake on the floor!